BUFORD
THE LITTLE
BIGHORN

Written and Illustrated by BILL PEET

HOUGHTON MIFFLIN COMPANY BOSTON

To Jan

Y 10 9 8 7

ISBN 0-395-20337-6 Reinforced Edition
ISBN 0-395-34067-5 Sandpiper Paperbound Edition

Buford was a scrawny little runt of a mountain sheep. Most of his growth had gone out the top of his head into a huge pair of horns. They went arching out over his back and on beyond him and still they weren't finished. Inch by inch and day by day they went curving onward while poor Buford worried. He was growing top-heavy and this could mean serious trouble to a mountain climber.

Like most bighorn sheep Buford belonged to a flock that travelled about the mountain tops where it was all ups and downs with jagged rocks, narrow ledges and steep cliffs. These sheep hardly ever worried about falling since they were all so nimble and sure-footed, that is everyone but the top-heavy Buford.

He came teetering and tottering along on shaky legs far behind all the others, and to the poor ram's dismay the top-heavy problem kept growing and growing. One day he discovered that his horns had taken a turn for the worse. They were heading his way!

"They're out to get me," thought Buford. "If they don't stop soon I'm sure to end up getting speared."

However, in a few months the horns grew on around him not even touching one hair of his hide, on past his legs, then on beyond his front feet to end up finally with a slight curl at the tips. The horn growing was finished but the damage was done. Now he must keep an eye on the cumbersome horns with every step for fear they might hook onto a ledge or catch in a cranny. Then there was always the danger of tripping over them.

"There's no doubt," grumbled the little ram, "but what these horns will be my downfall. One of these days they'll cause me to stumble and off the mountain I'll go."

And sure enough the horns did cause him to stumble and he toppled off a ledge to go tumbling down the mountainside.

Luckily for Buford, his horns hooked onto a snag of a spruce tree that stuck out from a crag. The horns had saved him from certain disaster. But then after all they were to blame for the fall.

The rest of the sheep were greatly alarmed by Buford's close call. From then on they pitched in to help. All the other rams took turns working as a team with two of them gripping his horns in their teeth while one gave Buford a big boost from below.

"How shameful," groaned the little bighorn, "to be so helpless and such a burden to my friends."

One morning as he was being hauled up a steep slope onto a flat table of rock, Buford decided he'd caused trouble enough.

"I can't let you help anymore," he said. "It's too much of a struggle, and besides it's not fair. So please go on your way and forget about me."

His friends stood around for a while looking sheepishly sad, and finally after wishing Buford the best of luck they went on their way. The unhappy little ram watched until the last of the sheep had disappeared over a distant ridge, then he turned his attention to the horns.

"I've got to get rid of these things," he muttered, "I'll knock them right off my head." And taking aim at a large boulder he went charging horns first like a battering ram. He hit with a jolting "Kerwham!" to go tumbling backward, his head spinning from the shock.

When at last he was able to see straight Buford discovered that the horns were still there as firmly rooted to his head as ever. "It's no use," he sighed, "these horns are mine for keeps. So I must figure out some way to live with them."

For a long time he stood on the edge of the bluff gazing into the valley far below. "It's mostly flat down there," thought Buford, "with no rocky ledges or steep drop-offs so maybe that's where I belong. Then if I tripped on my horns I'd get no more than a good bump on the nose."

To get there he must make the hazardous trip down the steep rugged mountainside, which seemed impossible with the horns in the way. Just the same Buford was going, and choosing a place where the rocks formed narrow stair steps, he began the dangerous descent.

Whenever he came to a place that seemed the least bit too steep he stopped until he found a safer easier way. Step by step he crept down the treacherous slope and by lunch time he had attracted a following of ravens and buzzards.

They expected the tottery unsteady ram to tumble most any minute, and they were all set to peck up the pieces on the jagged rocks far below. "If these birds get a free meal," muttered Buford, "it won't be on me, not if I can help it."

All afternoon the ram picked his way carefully down the steep mountainside, and without so much as one slip. Just before sundown he had reached the foot of the last rocky incline where the ground levelled off into a pine forest. The danger was past, and for the first time in his life Buford broke into a trot leaving the miserable ravens and buzzards perched in a pine.

It was such a relief to feel flat ground underfoot that he kept right on trotting all the way through the forest and out into a broad grassy meadow where someone was shouting. "Halt! Halt I say! Not one more step! Do you hear?"

A giant red bull followed by an army of bellowing cattle came lumbering toward the terrified bighorn. A beast from the forest could mean danger, and they crowded in shoulder to shoulder all set to charge at a word from their leader. After one close look the bull scoffed, "It's nothing but a runt of a mountain sheep all gone to horns. He's as harmless as a grasshopper."

With a few snorts of disgust the cattle ambled away into the meadow, and as the bull turned to go he said, "We'll not bother you, but there's no telling what the men might do." Buford had heard about men. Some of them killed things just for the fun of it. But right now he was much too weary to worry about anything. He sank to his knees, rolled over on his side, curled up in his horns, and in seconds he was snoring. It had been a long day.

Next morning Buford was awakened by a sputtering, coughing, rickety old jeep that came lurching to a stop by a water trough. A man jumped from the jeep and climbed up the tower for a look at the windmill. It was barely turning and yet there was a lively breeze. As the man leaned in to inspect the machinery the ram tiptoed quietly through the grass to slip in behind the nearest of the cattle.

There he remained stock still listening to the clanking of tools and the rusty squeaks of turning bolts. Pretty soon the windmill was whirling full tilt and the man went on his way. As the sputtering of the jeep faded into the distance the ram thought of a plan. After this he would keep well out of sight, and the huge herd of cattle would be his hideout.

Men made the rounds of the cattle ranch every few days. Buford could hear their shouting and laughter. Sometimes they came in the jeep and sometimes on horseback, never suspecting that the little big-horn was their guest for the summer. He was always well hidden somewhere near the center of the great milling herd, grazing lazily on the tall tender grass.

After the grass had withered away to wiry brown stubble the winter supply of hay was hauled in. There were heaping stacks of alfalfa on every part of the broad cattle range.

"This life is too easy, much too good to last," thought Buford, "sooner or later something will happen."

And sure enough one day something *did* happen.

It was a day in November, bleak and cold, and the rolling pasture land was white with the first snowfall. Buford was having breakfast with the cattle at one of the haystacks when over the wintery stillness came the steady humming of an airplane. Gradually the humming grew into a furious roar and the ram jerked his head up for a look.

The plane was circling over the field like a great bird of prey closing in on some helpless victim down below. Suddenly it came swooping over the haystack and Buford caught a flashing glimpse of two men in the plane. They were staring at him! These men were hunters! It was bighorn hunting season!

By the time the plane came gliding down to land on its skis at the far end of the field the ram was well on his way. He went galloping up through the pine forest, his horns leaving a deep-rutted trail as he went.

Buford was headed for the mountain tops where a blinding blizzard was howling. High up in the rocks the driving snow would wipe out his tracks, then he might give the hunters the slip. But his chances of getting there were slim indeed.

In this one-sided game the hunters always won. And as the two men came trudging up the ram's trail with their high-powered rifles set for a shot, they were grinning. This was their lucky day. The great pair of horns would break all hunting records with plenty to spare, and these grand trophies would be theirs in a matter of minutes.

With time running short Buford didn't dare stop to figure out the best way up the mountain. When he reached the first rocky incline he went scrambling up, grabbing onto a ledge with his forefeet and pulling himself up by the chin. Then in a frenzy of kicks he heaved himself up and over. Quickly he struggled to his feet and was about to continue the climb when he let out a cry of despair. He had blundered head-on into a steep granite wall!

The wall reared straight up fifty feet into the air. Poor Buford was in a panic. Now he had to climb back down and try another way up if only there were time.

First he had to find out if the hunters were coming and he leaned out over the ledge to peer down into the forest. Buford leaned out too far. He lost his footing and off he went!

The ram hit the soft snow to go rolling head over heels down the slope, his huge horns whirling like cartwheels. He bounced off a stump, took one big flip in mid air, and then to Buford's amazement. . . . .

. . . . he came down to land with all four feet planted squarely on his horns. And the horns were gliding over the slope exactly like skis heading straight for the hunters crouching below. There was no chance for a shot. The men leaped from the path of the onrushing ram to go sprawling headlong into the snow. And in a flash their prize bighorn was gone.

There was no way of steering the runaway skis, Buford was too busy fighting to keep his balance. The ram tottered from side to side, which sent the horns zigzagging crazily around rocks and logs and between trees in one near miss after another. He was heading back to the cattle ranch when the horns swerved sharply to the right up over a ridge and down a long slope where people were shouting. Lots of people!

He streaked past them so fast they were a blur of bright jackets and caps, and on down at the foot of the slope people were swarming like ants. There was no turning back! The bewildered bighorn went zooming straight into their midst to end up *Ker-floof!* in a great heap of snow.

At last Buford's luck had run out. He was trapped with no way to escape. The terrified ram couldn't bare to face the finish so he shut his eyes as the noisy crowd came closing in. Dozens of hands seized him by the horns to haul him out of the snow and he was lofted into the air.

As he was carried along, all at once the ram realized that this was a happy cheering crowd. These people weren't hunters, they were skiers like himself. This was a hero's welcome.

As suddenly as that Buford became the star attraction at the Little Big Pine winter resort. A special ski lift was rigged up for the remarkable ram, so there was no more struggling up steep slopes. It was all downhill from then on.

The little bighorn was surprisingly good for a beginner without any instruction. People came from such far away places as Oslo, Innsbruck, and Banff to see Buford. However, his skill as a skier wasn't the only reason for all the big crowds. They had come to see the one and only skier ever to grow his own skis.